J
636.8
NEY

Neye, Emily.

All about cats and
kittens.

ALL ABOUT
Cats and Kittens

Grosset & Dunlap

To Aunt Sue and Uncle Shep—E.N.
With love to Mum, you're the grandest tiger of all!—E.H.

Special thanks to Cape Cod Bengals and to the Falmouth Animal Hospital.

Photo credit p.6 Sphynx (Hairless), © Stephen Green-Armytage / Stock Market

Library of Congress Cataloging-in-Publication Data

Neye, Emily.
    All about cats and kittens / by Emily Neye ; photographs by Elizabeth Hathon.
      p. cm.—
Summary: Tells everything you want to know about America's most popular pet, including information about different breeds, how cats raise their kittens, and how you can care for your cat.
    1. Cats Juvenile literature. 2. Kittens Juvenile literature [1. Cats 2. Animals—Infancy. 3. Pets.]
I. Hathon, Elizabeth, ill. II. Title. III. Series: Grosset & Dunlap all aboard book.
  SF445.7.N49   1999
  636.8—dc21   99-35341
                                                      CIP

ISBN 0-448-42082-1   F G H I J

ALL ABOUT
Cats and Kittens

By Emily Neye

Photographs by Elizabeth Hathon

Grosset & Dunlap, Publishers

Did you know that cats are the most popular pets in the world?

It's easy to see why. Cats are smart, loyal, and affectionate. They also can be very entertaining!

Cats have lived with people for thousands of years—that's as long ago as the time of the ancient Egyptians! At first, people kept cats because they were so good at catching pesky rats and mice. But soon, people started liking cats for other reasons—the same reasons people love cats today. They make us smile. They keep us company. They are our friends.

Unlike dogs, most adult cats are about the same size and shape. But they can still look very different from one another. Some cats have short fur. Some have very fluffy fur. There are even some cats that don't have any fur at all!

Different types of cats, or *breeds*, have different kinds of coats. There are *shorthaired* breeds, like the Bengal. And there are *longhaired* breeds, like the Persian.

SPHYNX (HAIRLESS)

BENGAL

PERSIANS

Cats' coats come in many colors, too. They can be solid or patterned. A *tabby* cat has a striped or spotted coat. A *pointed* cat has ears, paws, tail, or face that are in different colors from the rest of its body.

Cats are experts at climbing and leaping. Their flexible bodies can twist and turn at amazing angles. And their long tails help them keep their balance.

This cat uses his strong hind legs to push off. Look how high he can leap! It's easy for him to reach his favorite hiding place.

Cats have no trouble walking along narrow fences and ledges. They are as graceful as the best tightrope walkers.

When cats do fall, they almost always land on their feet. While they are in the air, they twist their bodies and whip around their tails until their feet point downward. Cats don't think about doing this while they are falling. They are just following their instincts.

Cats are mammals, just like people. This means that after a mother cat gives birth to kittens, she feeds them milk from her body.

There are usually four or five kittens in a *litter*, or family. The newborns are tiny and helpless. When they are born, their eyes and ears are sealed shut. But their little noses are working! The kittens will depend on their sense of smell to find their mother's milk.

After about a week, their eyes and ears begin to open. And within three weeks, the kittens will begin to walk around and play. But they still need their mother for food and protection. This kitten has strayed too far away! Her mother lifts her up by the scruff of her neck to carry her back to her brothers and sisters.

Kittens from the same litter can be different colors. They can have different personalities, too. Some kittens are shy and some are frisky.

Did you know that every kitten is born with a different nose-print? Just like our fingerprints, no two nose-prints are alike!

Kittens need to stay with their mother for at least eight weeks after they are born. During that time, they grow and learn a lot. By watching their mother, they learn how to groom themselves. And by "play fighting" with each other, they learn how to hunt.

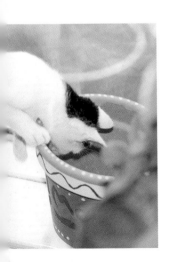

They also learn on their own—just like these curious kittens!

Young kittens shouldn't be adopted by human families right away. But they should have contact with people from the time they are about four weeks old. The more used to people they become, the better pets they will make.

Having a pet cat is a big responsibility. The kitten you bring home could be a part of your family for as long as twenty years! During that time, it will need lots of attention and love.

A young kitten should be fed four small meals every day. Older cats will probably only need one or two. Remember, cats need food made just for cats. Dog food and table food won't have all the nutrients your cat needs to stay healthy. Cool, fresh water should be available at all times, too.

Most cats love cream, like these two kittens! But it should be
given only as a special treat—too much can upset a cat's stomach.

If your cat is going to be kept indoors, you will need to train it to use a litter box. Cats are smart, so they usually catch on quickly. But be prepared for accidents!

You should keep the litter box in a quiet place, away from where your cat eats. Be sure to clean the box every day.

Cats clean themselves by licking their fur all over. Their rough tongues are covered with tiny spines—the spines work just like the teeth on a comb!

To clean its face, a cat licks its paw and then rubs it over its head.

But cats don't always groom themselves as well as they should. So they still need a regular brushing to get rid of loose hair and tangles. Longhaired cats, like Persians, need to be brushed at least once a day.

Just like you, your cat needs to visit the doctor for a checkup about once a year. Animal doctors are called *veterinarians.*

When you adopt a cat or kitten, you should take it to the veterinarian first thing—even before you take it home. The vet will make sure your cat is healthy and give it shots to protect it from diseases.

During checkups, the vet will examine your cat all over. He will look in your cat's ears. And he will listen to your cat's heartbeat.

A healthy cat should have a moist nose, clear eyes, clean ears, and a glossy coat. If you notice a change in the way your cat looks, you should take it to the veterinarian as soon as you can.

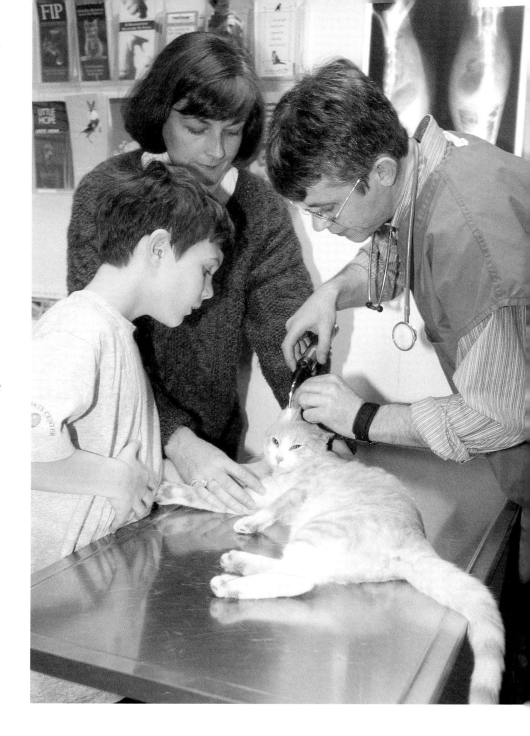

Cats need to exercise in order to stay fit, just like we do. Most cats don't like to be walked on leashes, but some don't mind!

As long as you have safe toys around, and make time to play together every day, your cat should stay trim.

A scratching post like this one works like a jungle gym, too. Not only will it keep cats busy, it also might save your furniture. All cats will scratch objects to stretch their legs and to keep their claws clean. So it's a good idea to train your cat to use a post, rather than the sofa!

Even though cats cannot speak, they can tell you how they are feeling in other ways.

A happy cat will purr and partially close its eyes.

An angry or scared cat will arch its back and puff up its fur, so it looks bigger. It may hiss or scream, too.

When a cat rubs up against you, it is saying, "We are family."

Cats have special glands around the face and near the base of the tail that produce odors. Even though cats may not smell strongly to us, they can tell one another apart with one sniff. By rubbing up against you, your cat marks you with its special scent. Now she, and other cats, will recognize you as part of her family.

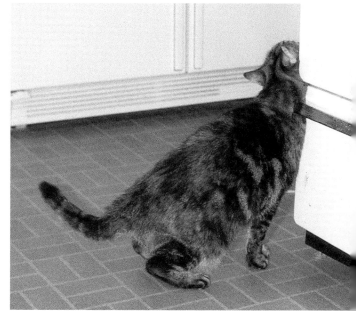

Cats mark their territory in the same way. When your cat rubs up against the furniture in your house, she is leaving behind a message to other animals. The message is: "This space belongs to me!"

You may notice that your cat spends a lot of its time dozing. Cats sleep up to sixteen hours a day! But they do not sleep for long stretches at one time. They just take short naps throughout the day and night. That's where the term "catnap" comes from.

Some people enter their cats in cat shows. A cat that is shown in a cat show must be *purebred*, which means its mother and father are of the same breed. There are forty-five official breeds in cat shows today.

The owners spend a lot of time preparing their cats. They are very proud.

Judges give a cat points for its coat, body, health, and personality.

This cat is a real champion— look at all the ribbons she has won!

But we don't need ribbons to tell us that our cats are special. They show us every day. Whether your cat is independent, playful, or shy, she is bound to be...

...full of surprises...

. . . and full of love.